方耀乾 著
Poems by Yaw-chien Fang

戴春馨 英譯
Translated by Chuen-shin Tai

尼琅菘 英文校訂
Revision by Jon Nichols

金色的曾文溪

The
Golden Zengwen River

方耀乾台漢英三語詩集

台灣詩叢 • Taiwan Poetry Series 18

【總序】詩推台灣意象

叢書策劃／李魁賢

　　進入二十一世紀，台灣詩人更積極走向國際，個人竭盡所能，在詩人朋友熱烈參與支持下，策畫出席過印度、蒙古、古巴、智利、緬甸、孟加拉、尼加拉瓜、馬其頓、秘魯、突尼西亞、越南、希臘、羅馬尼亞、墨西哥等國舉辦的國際詩歌節，並編輯《台灣心聲》等多種詩選在各國發行，使台灣詩人心聲透過作品傳佈國際間。

　　多年來進行國際詩交流活動最困擾的問題，莫如臨時編輯帶往國外交流的選集，大都應急處理，不但時間緊迫，且選用作品難免會有不週。因此，興起策畫【台灣詩叢】雙語詩系的念頭。若台灣詩人平常就有雙語詩集出版，隨時可以應用，詩作交流與詩人交誼雙管齊下，更具實際成效，對台灣詩的國際交流活動，當更加順利。

　　以【台灣】為名，著眼點當然有鑑於台灣文學在國際間名目不彰，台灣詩人能夠有機會在國際努力開拓空間，非為個人建立知名度，而是為推展台灣意象的整體事功，期待開創台灣文學的長久景象，才能奠定寶貴的歷史意義，台灣文學終必在世界文壇上佔有地位。

　　實際經驗也明顯印證，台灣詩人參與國際詩交流活動，很受重視，帶出去的詩選集也深受歡迎，從近年外國詩人和出版社與本人合作編譯台灣詩選，甚至主動翻譯本人詩集在各國文學雜誌或詩刊發表，進而出版外譯詩集的情況，大為增多，即可充分證明。

　　承蒙秀威資訊科技公司一本支援詩集出版初衷，慨然接受【台灣詩叢】列入編輯計畫，對台灣詩的國際交流，提供推進力量，希望能有更多各種不同外語的雙語詩集出版，形成進軍國際的集結基地。

故鄉佇我的心內閃爍

——序《金色的曾文溪》

方耀乾

　　《金色的曾文溪》是一本台語、漢語、英語三語的詩集，主要是咧書寫我的故鄉安定和我的家族。我共伊分做兩輯：（一）金色的故鄉、（二）卿卿如晤。

　　第一輯收錄有關描寫故鄉的詩作。我是台南安定海寮人，我佇遮出世、生長、受教育。國小我讀南安國小，國中讀安定國中，是故鄉晟養我、栽培我的。故鄉安定是一个農業鄉鎮，曾文溪箍過北爿面，隔溪的北岸就是西港，西爿、南爿和舊台南市相連，東爿和善化做厝邊，遙望東爿是美麗青翠的中央山脈。

　　安定原本屬平埔族西拉雅族目加溜灣社（Backloun）屬社直加弄社（Tackalan）的舊地，是台江內海的一个小貿易港，號做直加弄港。對阮這馬的庄頭地名就會當理解伊過去的地理環境和遺跡，譬如港口、港南、港仔尾、海寮、渡仔頭、頂洲仔、下洲仔、中崙仔、沙崙等。了後，曾文溪定定做大水，幾偌擺改道，並且沖入大量的泥沙，台江內海煞漸漸陸化，港口就慢慢喪失機能，轉變做純粹的農村。所致，如今的鄉民主要是以農為生。目前，安定的族群結構主要是台語人，民風樸實，人民單純實在。除了種稻仔和蕃薯以外，安定以出產西瓜、麻仔、蘆筍出名。毋過，佇工業和商業這方面，除了最近安定的西北角新設立的台積電18廠以外，區內差不多無啥大企業。這本詩集裡的詩作，我是以呵咾來懷念故鄉，以詩歌來記錄故鄉。

　　第二輯是有關描寫我的家族的詩作。我的家族佇十八世紀大清帝國乾隆坐位的時，對福建泉州同安渡過台灣海峽來到異鄉台灣移民開墾。如今異鄉已經成做新故鄉、新樂土。彼當時的新故鄉是倚海邊，所致名做海寮。阮的祖先刻苦耐勞認真拍拚，經過數代經營，到阮阿公方榮欽，已經歷六代。這本詩集主要書寫第六、七、八、九代家族的生活點滴和懷思：有我的阿公方榮欽、阿媽陳笑、阿爸方能安、阿母方富美、牽手戴錦綢、大漢查某囝方穎涵、細漢查某囝方穎萱。遮的詩是家族的記持，也是情感的抒發，更加是族群的傳承。所致我的筆觸風格也是溫馨的、懷舊的。

　　這本詩集會當出世出版，愛感謝詩人李魁賢（Kuei-shien Lee）的促成。另外，也愛感謝我的傑出學生戴春馨（Chuen-Shin Tai）博士，將本詩集翻譯做英文；也感謝尼琅菘（Jon Nichols）博士，協助訂正英文稿。目前您攏佇實踐大學應用英語系擔任助理教授。

——2021.12.18，63歲生日

目次

【一】金色的故鄉

金色的曾文溪

金色的黃昏髹[1]佇金色的曾文溪
Omar Khayyam[2]輕輕仔划出一首
微微仔醉
Sandro Botticelli[3] 將一幅春天
掛踮竹棑仔[4]
Demi的頭毛煞[5]向西天
飛出一隻火鳳凰
佇伊的目睭裡
我笑成一欉金黔紅[6]的莿桐花

---

[1] 髹：斜躺著小憩。
[2] Omar Khayyam（?-1123）：出生於波斯高拉森省的省會納霞堡，他是那個時代最有智慧的人之一，著有Rubáiyát（意為「四行詩」，台灣翻譯做《魯拜集》）。
[3] Sandro Botticelli（1445-1510）：義大利文藝復興時期的畫家，他最有名的畫作是「維納斯的誕生」，被認為是文藝復興精神的縮影。「春天」這幅畫充滿歡樂的氣息。
[4] 竹棑仔：竹筏。
[5] 煞：於是。
[6] 金黔（tòo）紅：金色透出紅色。

這个時陣　五分仔車[7]

載著甜甜的寄望

按黃昏的西港大橋喊喝[8]犁過

紫色的薊花[9]剪黏[10]佇

溪的兩爿[11]

黃色的鵝仔菜[12]爭咧舉手

相借問

金色的溪水

恬恬仔流向西

阮等待夜空

慢慢仔網起來

---

[7]　五分仔車：糖廠小火車。

[8]　喊喝（hiàm-huah）：吆喝。

[9]　紫色的薊（kè）花：即紫花薊香薊。初春，於原野開出紫色的小花。

[10]　剪黏：一種塑像的技巧。

[11]　兩爿（pîng）：兩邊。

[12]　鵝仔菜：即兔兒菜。為多年生草本菊科植物，春天開金黃色的花。

一暝的星
玎玎瑯瑯

2001/06/07，台南永康

【附記】曾文溪是嘉南平原上重要的溪流，流經過台南縣安定
鄉海寮村佮西港鄉的西港大橋的時景色上媠。以早，
日頭若斜西，橋頂時常有人咧留連，看夕照，這個景
色號稱做「曾橋晚照」。橋頂有一條小鐵枝路，若到
冬尾年初的時，時常會看著運送甘蔗的五分仔車對橋
頂駛過。這馬糖業稀微，鐵枝路也拆除。我佮Demi捌
散步過的溪流原在，西港大橋的車輛也來來去去，毋
過，橋頂的五分仔車、溪邊的莿桐花、紫花藿香薊、
鵝仔菜，干焦佇春天溫柔的風裡，搖成一蕊一蕊甜蜜
的記持。

金色的故鄉安定

金色的故鄉安定
是遮爾仔[13]美麗
藍色的天，白色的雲
甜蜜的空氣，彩色的花海
景緻繽紛真多彩

金色的故鄉安定
物產真豐富
春天割蘆筍、熱天挽西瓜
秋天割稻仔、寒天kheh麻油[14]
上天慈愛有保庇

金色的故鄉安定
我欲呵咾[15]你

---

[13] 遮爾仔：這麼的。
[14] kheh麻油：榨麻油。
[15] 呵咾（o-ló）：讚美。

溪水彎彎流過北斗，像阿母溫柔的懷抱
稻田遍地黃金閃爍，像阿爸慈愛咧守護
使我癡迷沉醉

透早露水掖佇咱安定
遍地是金爍爍的珍珠
黃昏日頭照佇曾文溪
一條七彩的黃金花毯

我的故鄉安定
你是母親
我欲呵咾你
我的故鄉安定
你是父親
我欲感激你

2021/10/01，台南永康

思念故鄉

——海寮

摘[16]一片夕陽
貼踮[17]普陀寺的飛簷
四分之一世紀進前的記憶之盒
齊光起來[18]
觀世音菩薩慈眉釣起塵封的往事
靠底[19]的童年
開始輕輕仔咧划船

歲月洄游親像溯源的魩仔魚[20]
阿爸舉鋤頭的姿勢宛若生龍活虎
阿母幼綿綿的雙手刻出榕仔的風霜

---

[16] 摘：音tiah，揀取。
[17] 貼踮：貼在。
[18] 齊（tsiâu）光起來：整個全亮了起來。
[19] 靠底（khò-té）：擱淺。
[20] 魩（but）仔魚：一種小魚，台灣人愛用來煮粥，或勾芡。與鮭魚相同溯源產卵，過程艱辛，令人動魄。

彼年割香的陣頭鑼鼓喧天
拚場的布袋戲佮歌仔戲是啥得著頭綵

風吹過十二月的甘蔗園
我的童年曝佇蔗葉
　　　曝佇牛車
　　　曝佇火車

風吹過九月的稻埕
我的鄉愁鑲黃金
　　　鑲南風
　　　鑲日頭

假使童年會當慢慢仔哺[21]
一定是甜甜芳芳

---

[21] 哺（pōo）：咀嚼。

我咬過的西瓜
猶倒佇溪埔咧睏
我划過的竹桸仔
猶佇曾文溪等我出帆
我的跤跡一直晾²²佇蘆筍園
毋甘轉來
聽講大箍福仔咧做大頭家
矮仔勝咧起大樓
愛哭英仔咧做幼稚園的園長

故鄉是一矸用鄉愁寬寬仔²³激出來的酒
逐喙都予汝
醉茫茫

2000/11/27，台南女子技術學院

---

22 晾：音nê，晾曬。
23 寬（khuann）寬仔：慢慢的。

【附記】海寮屬台南縣安定鄉，是一個靠曾文溪的莊頭，村民差不多攏姓方，種作的農作物主要有西瓜、小玉仔、蘆筍、稻仔、蕃薯等。莊頭中心有一座廟叫做普陀寺，主要奉祀楊府太師，後來增加觀音佛祖。海寮是西港慶安宮的香境（俗稱西港仔香），楊府太師位居左先鋒，有組南管陣頭參加割香。

19

海寮方惡甲無人問

這句俗語自細漢就佇我的心肝底
閃袂離[24]的刺
哪會遮爾衰[25]
我拄好[26]蹛[27]海寮閣[28]姓方
倒看正看
我攏是[29]遮爾仔溫純兼古意
遠看近看
海寮人攏遮爾仔拍拚閣好鬥陣[30]
阿公講做人愛照紀綱[31]
阿媽講囡仔人愛用功讀冊

---

[24] 閃袂離：躲不開。
[25] 遮爾衰（tsiah-nī sue）：這麼倒楣。
[26] 拄好：剛好。
[27] 蹛（tuà）：住。
[28] 閣（koh）：又。
[29] 攏是：都是。
[30] 好鬥陣：好相處。
[31] 照紀綱：按照道理行事。

阿爸講做代誌[32]愛拍拚

阿母講咱愛人人好

我攏有聽

有一工[33]有一個人

共我譬相[34]海寮人

查甫的[35]上無情

查某的[36]上無義

我氣甲共伊揍[37]

我才知影[38]海寮方實在有夠惡

我才知影海寮方實在有夠惡

2001/06/09，台南永康

---

[32] 代誌：事情。

[33] 一工：一天。

[34] 譬相（phì-siònn）：指尖酸刻薄的批評。

[35] 查甫的：男人。

[36] 查某的：女人。

[37] 揍（bok）：用拳頭打人。

[38] 知影：知道。

【附記】海寮屬台南縣安定鄉，是一个靠曾文溪的庄頭，村民
　　　　大多數姓方。自細漢定定聽人講起「海寮方惡甲無
　　　　人問」。起初毋知是何意，干焦知是咧譬相海寮人真
　　　　歹。後來慢慢才知伊的緣由：海寮人歹是因為當予外
　　　　人欺負到忍無可忍的時，海寮人會全村團結抵抗，所
　　　　以予人有真歹的印象。另外，猶閣一句講法「海寮方
　　　　惡甲無尻川」。

蘇厝

——王船的故鄉

船底的金紙點著[39]
火煙慢慢仔衝懸
火是浪　煙是風
出帆囉　出帆囉
民眾用虔誠的心
告別王船
王船佇大火當中
佇煙霧當中
寬寬仔[40]勻勻仔[41]出帆
告別王爺
感恩恁代天巡狩庇佑
瘟疫速速離開
COVID-19速速逃亡
恁選擇淳樸的蘇厝

---

[39] 點著（tiám-toh）：點火、把燈點亮。
[40] 寬寬仔（khuann-khuann-á）：慢慢地、謹慎小心地。
[41] 勻勻仔（ûn-ûn-á）：慢慢地、謹慎小心地。

暫蹛[42]

阮用感恩的心

守護王船

阮起兩間大廟

奉祀王爺

台灣上早的王船祭

從此啟幕

三年一科做醮又閣到矣

敬請王爺上船

曾文溪水青青

王船寬寬仔向西出帆

金紙若山疊懸懸[43]

王船輕輕向天飛起

瘟疫啊！速速

離開

2021/10/04，台南永康

---

[42] 蹛（tuà）：住。

[43] 懸懸（kuân-kuân）：高高的。

佮沈光文夜談

我熟似⁴⁴你
佇你過身了後三百外冬
咱不時佇暗暝相約
阮兜開講
你的目頭結一蕊烏雲
「歲歲思歸思不窮」
「夢裡家鄉夜夜還」
我想我會當了解
佇目加溜灣西爿⁴⁵的海垺
夜星含著珠淚
你將鄉愁輕輕仔掖踮⁴⁶海裡

佇2002年的台南
我想欲拆機票

---

⁴⁴ 熟似（sik-sāi）：認識、熟識。
⁴⁵ 西爿（sai-pîng）：西邊。
⁴⁶ 掖踮（iā-tiàm）：灑在。

予你飛轉去
三百外冬前
夢中的鄞縣
夢中的某団
只是　只是
你敢會像
80、90年代的老榮民
相見不如莫見
閣飛倒轉來
熟似的異鄉
台灣

我出世佇安定鄉
以早你教冊行醫的所在
阮的祖先一定有受著
你的啟蒙
你教愿愛土地愛別人

這嘛是阮 Siraya 的優良傳統

你寫跤踏的風土

這嘛是阮拍拚書寫的對象

你寫足濟鄉愁的詩

我想啥人無鄉愁呢

你有故鄉毋過無國家通倒轉去

我有故鄉卻是猶無家己的國家

佮你仝款

阮的目頭常在結一蕊烏雲

2002/09/21，台南永康
九二一台灣地動三週年紀念日

【附記】沈光文（1612-1688），字文開，號斯庵，浙江鄞縣
　　　　（今之寧波）人，南明時代擔任工部郎佮太僕少卿。
　　　　鄭成功據守廈門、金門的時，本底想欲對金門坐船前
　　　　往泉州，後遇風颱漂流至台灣。晚年居目加溜灣社
　　　　（今之台南縣善化佮安定）教冊授徒。在台歷經荷、

鄭、清三國。伊是第一個將漢文化帶來台灣的人，並
且佇1685年創立台灣第一個詩社「東吟社」，被尊為
「海東文獻初祖」、「開台文化祖師」、「台灣第一
士大夫」、「台灣孔子」。著有〈台灣輿圖考〉、
〈草木雜記〉、〈流寓考〉、〈台灣賦〉、《文開詩
文集》，龔顯宗編有《沈光文全集及其研究資料彙
編》（1998，台南：縣立文化中心）。Siraya著是活動
佇台南、高雄、屏東的平埔族。

公厝

熱天的燒氣，猶停留佇公埕[47]。夜色佮燒氣咧談判。南海佛祖半瞇的目睭，若咧入定。香芳味對三百冬的香爐淒出來，哦，三百冬的芳味寫著故鄉的氣味、祖先一步一步血汗的跤跡。歷代祖先捌佇伊的四周圍行過。拜過神明了後，阿祖、阿公、阿媽、阿爸、阿母攏捌佇這个香爐插過香。佇衝懸香火煙中，我看見愓的形影，佇公厝[48]內來來去去，笑面向我講話。

2016/09/11，台南永康

---

[47] 公埕：庄頭廟的廟埕。
[48] 公厝：庄頭廟。佇遮指台南市安定區海寮的普陀寺，我故鄉的公廟。

五分仔車[49]

聽著「嘟──嘟──」，十歲的童年轉來，甘蔗的童年轉來。

彼年，一枝一枝的甘蔗是阿爸阿母一張一張的銀票，一張一張會笑出聲的銀票。

彼年，一枝一枝的甘蔗是阮一个一个的夢，一个一个甜甜的夢。

風吹佇甘蔗，甘蔗頂歇一、兩隻烏秋，烏秋的烏是糖廠的煙筒，煙筒徛踮火車頭，「嘟──」一聲是糖的童年。

2000/11/19，台南永康

---

[49] 五分仔車：糖廠運甘蔗的小火車。

行啊行

行啊行，行啊行，我一直行一直行。我對我的故鄉台南海寮出發，行到天邊海角。對日出行到日落；對星浮行到星落；對庄跤行到都市；對平洋行到深山；對山邊行到海垺；對春天行到夏天；對秋天行到冬天。佇雨中行、佇風中行、佇雪中行。我一直行，一直行，一直行，一直行。欲去看這个世界、去聽這个世界、去鼻這个世界、去摸這个世界、去啖這个世界。

2020/01/01，元旦，台南鳳凰山莊

故鄉，載我轉去祖靈的禮車

曾文溪南，春天的番薯共芳貢貢貯滇我的心肝窟仔，熱天
的溪埔厚汁的西瓜佮青幼的蘆筍倒咧睏，秋天的菅芒舞動
著白色的波浪，寒天的蔗園有甜甜的記持。彼是台南縣安
定鄉一個靠曾文溪南岸的小庄頭，叫做海寮，是我源起頭
肉體的紅瓦厝。

兩百年前，海寮徛佇台江內海的岸邊。三百年前，海寮是
西拉雅族直加弄社掠魚的田園。我敢若看見高強的查甫祖
手舉長槍射梅花鹿的姿勢，長長的頭毛飛起來，隨在南風
輕輕梳頭，也敢若聽見美麗的查某祖吹著美妙的喙琴，琴
聲褸過台江內海的波浪星光。故鄉，是載我肉體的禮車，
轉去祖靈。

2005/06/10，台南永康

【二】卿卿如晤

古冊行出來的隱者

——予阿公方榮欽（1902-1975）

像咒語，你的喙咧吟詩句
若密語，你的喙咧哼南管
佇貓霧光[1]中，佇黃昏裡
你抱琵琶
啊！遮爾熟悉又閣遐爾生份的形象
你是對神秘的古冊行出來的隱者

早起，洗盪[2]了後
您慣勢[3]散一下仔步
吃過清糜醬菜
坐佇看診室的籐椅
招喚患者入診間望聞問切
你是一个為病患把脈的良醫

---

[1] 貓霧光（bâ-bū-kng）：曙光出現時的光亮。
[2] 洗盪（sé-tng）：洗滌、清洗。
[3] 慣勢（kuàn-si）：習慣。

欲睏進前，和你倒佇眠床
你照慣例嚨喉⁴清清咧開始講囡仔古
虎姑婆的恐怖
佮林投姐的不幸
是我文學的啟蒙
你是一个講故事的慈祥阿公

當時才會當閣再聽一首你吟的古詩？
當時才會當閣再聽一曲你彈的琵琶？
當時才會當閣再聽你講一擺囡仔古？

2021/09/27，台南永康

---

⁴　嚨喉（nâ-âu）：喉嚨。

懷念你，佇相片內

——致阿媽陳笑（1904-1966）

干焦會當佇相片內
走揣你的溫暖和愛
你過身的時我7歲
我竟然對你無半點記持
干焦會當看彼幾年
你和我的合照

台北新公園裡
我圍著頭巾，你攬我
天親像有淡薄仔冷，落著微微仔雨
涼亭邊的杜鵑花盛開
閣再來是圓山動物園
我和猶真勇壯的大象林旺合照呢
猶閣有彼頷頸長長的長頷鹿苑春
哦，佇野柳
女王成做咱的背景
海浪的聲音親像

對相片裡溢出來
就按呢
按呢而已

凡勢佇南部的家鄉
你捌炁我踏遍海寮的稻浪
甘蔗收成的時
你捌削甘蔗予我止喙焦
也捌佇灶空裡焄番薯
解我的飢
毋過我竟然
竟然攏記袂起來

下暗我欲藉著相片
和您相會　思念你
遙想你
走揣你的溫暖和愛

2021/11/01，台南永康

雺霧中

——予父親方能安（1925-1982）

我艘過記憶的雺霧
拼貼你的形影
你騎川崎機車
模樣真緣投
我坐佇機車的油箱頂
心情真是樂暢
迎著微風，路樹向後飛過
看這原野，稻穗黚著黃金
啊！日頭真正是燦爛
啊！空氣真正是清新

紲落來，是中年的你
看診室充滿著藥水味
桌頂的聽筒若像會當聽見
世間的真濟秘密
病人坐佇看診室外面的長椅
時鐘滴滴答答講著

漸漸褪色的人生
「5號李先生！」
李先生面帶痛苦進到看診室
我聽毋捌恁講的話
時鐘猶閣咧滴滴答答
你佇藥單寫一寡字

接落來，是晚年的你
雙跤腫甲若蒜頭的關節，
你行的每一條路攏是
刀路啊！
每一个微微顫的跤步
攏是刀劃針搣
關節裡飽滿的蒜頭
內面攏是白白的石灰
半夜哀叫聲

風中目眉結肉球
成做我耳裡眼中的風景

彼工你斷氣
佇左營海軍總病院
我揀著你的遺體
行過長長的走廊
夕陽照著你
青黃的面容
消瘦的跤手
是你最後的遺像

到今夢你你無來
明仔載夢中你敢會來

2021/06/26，台南永康

阮阿母是太空人

一九六九年七月二十日
阿姆斯壯
穿太空衫
揹氧氣筒
行佇月娘頂面　講出
驚天動地的話：
「雖然是我的一小步
毋過，是人類的一大步」
自彼陣開始，我就暗暗
種一个夢
向望做一个太空人

二十八冬後
我的夢
無莩芛
無釘根
阮阿母煞變做太空人

嘛穿太空衫
嘛揹氧氣筒
月娘變做病房
伊一小步嘛無半步
免講是一大步

這陣我閣再
種一个夢
向望阮阿母莫做太空人

1997/12/19，台南永康

【附註】阮阿母對一九九六年正月初四中風到現此時已經兩冬
半矣，無法度坐，無法度待，無法度行，規工倒佇病床
頂。家己亦袂曉翻身，嘛袂曉食物件佮喘氣，著愛鬥胃
管佮呼吸器。這首詩共伊叫做〈阮阿母是太空人〉，是
因為阮阿母愛鬥呼吸器佮胃管才會當維持伊的性命，伊
的模樣佮揹氧氣筒、鬥呼吸器的太空人全款。

阿母的皮包

細漢的時
阿母的皮包仔是
一跤寶箱
有糖仔佮餅仔
有胭脂嘛有水粉

大漢的時
阿母的皮包仔是
一跤藥箱
有胃散佮萬金油
有高血壓的藥仔嘛有救心

這馬
阿母的皮包仔是
一張病床
囥伊烏凋瘦的身軀
嘛囥阮沉重的心情

1998/07/13，台南永康

阿母，你無乖

——予母親方富美（1926-2001）

阿母，你無乖
自細漢你叫阮著愛乖

「飯愛食較濟咧
大漢通做大代誌」
「身體著愛振動
跤手勇健才會行出你的春天」
「意志著愛堅強
拍拼你的光明前程」

阿母，你無乖
你　飯食一喙喙仔
你　跤手無愛振動
你　意志嘛無堅強
阮　愛予你佮阮做伙做大代誌
阮　愛予你佮阮鬥陣行出咱的春天
阮　愛予你看著咱的光明前程

毋過
阿母，你無乖

1997/12/04，台南永康

【附註】母親晚年中風，無法度家己行動，也無法度家己食物
件，干焦規工倒佇眠床。

欲去看阿母

若是大好天
我著會去阿里山
看山櫻弄春天
毋過今仔日
我欲去看阿母

若是落雨天
我著會去烏山頭
看雨水吟歌詩
毋過今仔日
我欲去看阿母

若是日頭火燒埔
我著會去鵝鑾鼻
佮海湧跳曼波
毋過今仔日
我欲去看阿母

若是凍霜的寒天
我著會踮厝內
佮牽手談戀愛
毋過今仔日
我欲去看阿母

這馬阿母踮佇病院

1998/05/27，台南永康

春天佗位去

上冊愛的是草山的杜鵑
阮驚看著伊紅膏赤蟮⁵的形影
上冊愛的是白河的蓮花
阮驚看著伊粉妝打扮的嬌容
上冊愛的是草嶺的菅芒
阮驚看著伊舞動秋風的姿勢
上冊愛的是楠西的梅花
阮驚看著伊無畏霜雪的花蕊

杜鵑有伊的春天
蓮花有伊的夏天
菅芒有伊的秋天
梅花有伊的冬天
阿母，我問你

---

⁵　紅膏赤蟮（âng-ko-tshiah-tshih）：臉色紅潤，形容身體健康。

你的春天
佗位去

1997/12/15，台南永康

父女的祈禱

細漢查囝上愛拜拜
看著寺廟著欲拜
焄伊去中醫館看病
伊講欲去媽祖廟拜拜
欲拜阿媽的病趕緊好起來

媽祖　媽祖
聽阿爸咧講
你上慈悲
你上疼囝仔紅嬰
我共你拜
你著愛保庇我的阿媽
病較緊好起來
媽祖　媽祖
你千萬毋通袂記

媽祖娘娘
弟子方耀乾
蹛[6]佇永康市
點香來共你拜
一無欲求名
二無欲求利
三無欲求位
只求弟子的阿娘
安享天年
只求弟子的厝內大細
平安好勢

出來到廟埕斗
一面想一面越頭[7]
三百外冬來

6　蹛（tuà）：居住。
7　越頭（uat-thâu）：回頭。

伊一直看顧台灣這个所在
阮嘛向望伊繼續照顧阮一家口

1998/07/26,台南永康

羊蹄甲若發燒

羊蹄甲若發燒
春天著到
阮的心內著
唱歌詩
阮會佮伊相對看
看甲阮兩人發燒

羊蹄甲若發燒
春天著到
阮的心內著
出日頭
阮會佮伊坐佇樹仔跤
共公園坐甲發燒

羊蹄甲若發燒
春天著到
阮的心內著

出彩虹
阮會牽著伊的手
共街仔路踏甲發燒

羊蹄甲若發燒
春天著到
阮的心內著
開花
阮欲佇每一個人的心內種一欉花
予每一個人發燒

1998/03/31，台南永康

【附記】羊蹄甲屬蘇木科落葉喬木，春天開花，原產地是中國
俗印度，葉片像羊蹄，葉仔鈍而圓，表面有帶粉質，
葉脈無偌明顯，花色像洋蘭，粉紅色，果子是豆莢
狀。春天的時，佇台灣四界攏看會著。

伊咧等我

艋舺[8]親像箭
射過金色的相思海
風的翼親像伊的喙
唚著我的面
猛掠[9]的麻虱目[10]
佇金色的水裡走標[11]
伊講麻虱目是愛情的符仔
一定愛載一船轉去
下暗佇竹抱跤通佮伊
配月光吞落去

我一定愛載一船轉去
伊一定佇岸邊

---

[8] 艋舺（bangka）：小船、獨木舟。平埔族西拉雅語。
[9] 猛掠（mé-liah）：（動作）敏捷。
[10] 麻虱目：虱目魚。古早台江內海出產麻虱目。
[11] 走標（tsáu-pio）：賽跑。

西照日點著伊的目睭
若兩蕊熱情的火堆
等我

我一定愛載一船轉去
伊一定佇岸邊
Cocoa的皮膚金滑柔軟
飽滇的胸前開兩蕊圓仔花
等我

我一定愛載一船轉去
下暗佮伊
溶做月光
佇竹抱跤

2005/09/03，台南永康

歌

——予Demi

用我上深情的目睭
共你看做一幅油畫

用我上利[12]的兩蕊耳
共你聽做一首夜曲

用我上認真的鼻仔
共你鼻做一罐芳水

用我上熱情的喙[13]唇
共你唚[14]做一束玫瑰

用我上溫柔的雙手
共你塑做一尊琉璃

---

[12] 上利（lāi）：最靈敏。

[13] 喙（tshuì）唇：嘴唇。

[14] 唚（tsim）：吻。

最後
用我上讚嘆的心
共你讀做一欉柳樹
佮一欉榕仔[15]

1995/03/29，華語初稿
1998，台語定稿佇永康

---

[15] 榕仔（tshîng-á）：榕樹。

三十一冬後的噗仔聲

——予牽手Demi

彼年你的模樣
我想我猶會記得
你十一歲
我嘛十一歲
咱讀仝班　南安國小五年忠班
第一擺見面　應該是佇九月

你無偌大漢
瘦瘦的一个查某囡仔嬰
頭毛留到耳仔邊
褪赤跤　細細支的跤
恬恬　有兩蕊倔強的
目睭

汝冊讀了袂穤
定定一枝鉛筆寫甲
賰一節仔

拎佇細細支的手裡
搝力咧犁簿仔紙

厝裡無故事冊通看
學校圖書室的冊
攏予你借了了
〈賣番仔火的查某囡仔〉
常在佇透風落雨的暗暝
予你想起猶有媽媽的溫暖

後來聽人講
畢業彼一年
你是全校第一名
袂當領上懸的獎
縣長獎是欲予彼个
老師的後生

61

畢業典禮彼這工
毋捌穿過鞋的你
細細支的跤蹄
穿一雙共阿媽借的鞋
傷大跤的鞋
上台領第二獎
一步　噗
　　　一步　噗
　　　　　一步　噗
　　　　　　　一步　噗
Peh上台仔頂
彼陣麻黃仔徛甲恬唧唧
蟬仔佇校園內大聲抗議

2002/10/14，台南永康

你的目頭結一蕊憂愁

下暗你又閣比我較早睏
無共我講：暗安
我覕佇你的身軀邊
咧看家己主編　才出版的
《台語文學讀本》
敧頭共你看
烏齾齾的長頭鬃掖佇枕頭
共白泡泡的面抱咧
我捌輕輕仔拈過的鼻仔
勻勻仔咧呼吸人間歲月
我捌唚過的喙誠無辜
恬恬無講話
兩蕊大蕊重巡的目晭這時瞌瞌
目睫毛溫柔咧看顧一暝的眠夢
這個面嫁予我20冬
佇我的心目中
一直是一個美麗的瓷仔

這陣目頭結一蕊憂愁

我共冊园跖胸前
溫柔的燈光
將我的手鉸做一個影
欲共掰予平
毋過憂愁隨閣結起來
我的手挲過你的
頭額
　　目眉
　　　　鬢邊
　　　　　　喙頓

佇溫暖恬靜的眠床頂
我開始思考憂愁的哲學
是毋是上班傷忝
是毋是身體無爽快

是毋是操煩查某囝
抑是我愛汝的電無夠

二十冬前
你將你交予我
我暗暗共家己講
無欲予烏暗靠近你
真明顯　我失約
胸前的《台語文學讀本》滑落眠床跤
我倒落眠床將你的手牽咧
汝目頭的憂愁
一直渧
　　　一直渧
渧到我的目頭

2003/02/22，台南永康永二街

南方的鳳凰花，向前行

——予涵

抱著祝福的心情
欲共你的希望加分
雖然武林高手齊到
徛予在
心頭定
有信心就會贏

台北激一個
冷冷的面腔[16]
宛然武林高手
冷冷的心胸
台大陽明論劍
毋免必死的決心
愛有奮戰的精神

---

[16] 面腔（bīn-tshiunn）：面貌。指看起來親切或兇惡的臉色，而不是美醜。

你是南方熱情的鳳凰花
輸贏攏愛堅強面對

牽著汝的手
佇台北街頭
親像過去十七冬
我燒滾滾的手欲共你的信心
燃[17]予燒
我勇健健的手欲共你的意志
䂹[18]予勇
欲共你焄入去戰場
干焦火煉才會變成金
干焦焠煉才會變成鋼
南方的鳳凰花

---

[17] 燃（hiânn）予燒：燒熱。

[18] 䂹（khōng）：以水泥或磚頭砌磚、牆等，使之如水泥般堅固。

自你去
向前行
爸爸永遠支持你

2000/03/26，寫佇台北回台南的莒光號火車內

【附記】陪大漢查某囝上台北參加台大（3/24-3/25）、陽明
（3/26）醫學系申請入學考試，有感而寫。這馬將這
首詩拍入電腦的時，已經知也伊考牢陽明醫學系矣。

查某囝的「國語」考卷

——予萱

查某囝一面行一面吼轉來
老師罵伊烏白亂寫
考試單仔頂面一粒大鴨卵

造句：
1.……有時……有時……
答：我們老師有時會罵人，有時會打人。
2.……中秋……
答：一年四季當中秋天最美麗。
3.……會……不會……
答：我爸爸說：總統　蔣公會大便，不會講台語。
4.一朵朵……
答：一朵朵的綿羊在天空游泳。
5.……綠油油……
答：春天把草原綠油油了。

是佗跡毋著，查某囝問我
因為你是詩人，我回答

1999/01/21，台南永康

漢語篇

故鄉在我心中閃爍

——序《金色的曾文溪》

方耀乾

　　《金色的曾文溪》為台語、漢語、英語三語詩集，主要在書寫我的故鄉安定和我的家族。我將之分為兩輯：（一）金色的故鄉、（二）卿卿如晤。

　　第一輯收錄有關描寫故鄉的詩作。我是台南安定海寮人，我在這裡出生、生長、受教育。國小我就讀南安國小，國中就讀安定國中，是故鄉養育了我、栽培了我。故鄉安定是一個農業鄉鎮，曾文溪在北邊蜿蜒迤邐，隔著溪的北岸就是西港，西邊、南邊和舊台南市相連，東邊和善化互為鄰居，遙望東邊是美麗青翠的中央山脈。

　　安定原本屬平埔族西拉雅族目加溜灣社（Backloun）屬社直加弄社（Tackalan）的舊地，是台江內海的一個小貿易港，稱做直加弄港。我們從現在的村落地名就可理解她過去的地理環境和遺跡，譬如港口、港南、港仔尾、海寮、渡仔頭、頂洲仔、下洲仔、中崙仔、沙崙等。之後，曾文溪常常氾濫，數次改道，並且沖入大量的泥沙，台江內海漸漸陸化，港口遂喪失機能，轉變為純粹的農村。所致，如今的鄉民主要是以農為生。目前，安定的族群結構主要是台語人，民風樸實，人民單純實在。除了種植稻米和蕃薯以外，安定以出產西瓜、芝麻、蘆筍出名。不過，在工業和商業上，除了最近安定的西北角新設立的台積電18廠以外，區內幾無大企業。這本詩集裡的詩作，我以讚美來懷念故鄉，以詩歌來記憶故鄉。

　　第二輯有關描寫我的家族的詩作。我的家族於十八世紀大清帝國乾隆時期，從福建泉州同安強渡台灣海峽來到異鄉台灣移民開墾。如今異鄉已成為新故鄉、新樂土。斯時的新故鄉位於海邊，故名為海寮。祖先們胼手胝足披荊斬棘，歷經數代經營，至我祖父方榮欽，已歷六代。這本詩集主要書寫第六、七、八、九代家族的生活點滴和懷思：我的祖父方榮欽、祖母陳笑、父親方能安、母親方富美、妻子戴錦綢、大女兒方穎涵、小女兒方穎萱。它是家族的記憶，也是情感的抒發，更是族群的傳承。因此我的筆觸風格也是溫馨的、懷舊的。

　　這本詩集能夠問世出版，要感謝詩人李魁賢（Kuei-shien Lee）的促成。另也要感謝我的傑出學生戴春馨（Chuen-Shin Tai）博士將本詩集翻譯成英文；朋友尼琅菘（Jon Nichols）博士，協助訂正英文稿。春馨和尼琅菘目前在實踐大學應用英語系擔任助理教授。

——2021.12.18，63歲生日

目次

【一】金色的故鄉

金色的曾文溪

金色的黃昏躺臥在金色的曾文溪

Omar Khayyam[1]輕輕的划出一首

微醺

Sandro Botticelli[2]將一幅春天

掛在竹筏上

Demi的秀髮向西天

飛出一隻火鳳凰

在她的眼眸裡

我笑成一株金鑲紅的莿桐花

這個時候　五分車[3]

---

[1] Omar Khayyam（?-1123）：生於波斯高拉森省的省會納霞堡，為他那個時代最有智慧的人之一，著有*Rubáiyát*（意為「四行詩」）。

[2] Sandro Botticelli (1445-1510)：義大利文藝復興時期的畫家，其最廣為人知的畫作是「維納斯的誕生」，被認為是文藝復興精神的縮影。「春天」一畫充滿歡樂的氣息。

[3] 五分車：為臺灣糖業鐵路，地方上稱為五分仔車，是為配合臺灣

載著甜甜的寄望
從黃昏的西港大橋吆喝犁過
紫色的薊花[4]剪黏[5]在
溪的兩旁
黃色的兔兒菜[6]爭著舉手
打招呼
金色的溪水
靜靜的流向西

我們等待夜空
慢慢的網起
一夜的星星
玎玎璫璫

2001/06/07，台南永康

糖業需要而興建的專用鐵路。通常以運送甘蔗、原料為主。
[4]　紫色的薊花：即紫花薔香薊。初春，於原野開出紫色的小花。
[5]　一種塑像的技巧。在此用為動詞。
[6]　兔兒菜為多年生草本菊科植物，春天開金黃色的花。

【附記】曾文溪是嘉南平原最重要的溪流,流經台南市安定區
海寮和西港區西港大橋這地帶的時候景緻最為美麗。
以前,每當夕陽斜西,橋上時常有人留連,觀賞夕
照,這個美景稱做「曾橋晚照」。橋上有一條糖廠小
鐵路,每到冬天的時候,時常會看著運送甘蔗的五分
車從橋上駛過。如今糖業沒落,鐵路也被拆除。我和
Demi曾散步過的溪流原在,西港大橋的車輛也還來來
往往,不過,橋上的五分車、溪邊的莿桐花、紫花藿
香薊、兔兒菜,只能在春天的微風裡,搖成一朵朵甜
蜜的回憶。

金色的故鄉安定

金色的故鄉安定
是這麼的美麗
藍藍的天空、白白的雲朵
甜蜜的氣息、彩色的花海
景緻繽紛真多彩

金色的故鄉安定
物產真豐饒
春天割蘆筍、夏天採西瓜
秋天割稻子、冬天榨芝麻
上天慈愛又庇佑。

金色的故鄉安定
我要讚美你
溪水蜿蜒環繞北邊，像母親溫柔的懷抱
稻田遍地閃爍黃金，像父親慈愛的守護
真令我癡迷陶醉

清晨露珠灑在安定鄉
遍地佈滿晶瑩的珍珠
黃昏陽光照在曾文溪
一條蜿蜒的黃金花毯

我的故鄉安定
您是母親，
我要讚美妳
我的故鄉安定
您是父親，
我要感謝你。

2021/10/01，台南永康

思念故鄉

——海寮

摘一片夕陽
貼在普陀寺的飛簷
四分之一世紀前的記憶之盒
全亮了起來
觀世音菩薩的慈眉釣起塵封的往事
擱淺的童年
開始輕輕的划起船

歲月洄游如溯源的魩仔魚[7]
阿爸舉起鋤頭的姿勢依然是生龍活虎
阿母幼綿綿的雙手刻劃出榕樹的風霜
那年刈香的陣頭鑼鼓喧天
拚場的布袋戲和歌仔戲是誰得到頭綵

風吹過十二月的甘蔗園

---

[7] 魩（but）仔魚：一種小魚，台灣人愛用來煮粥，或勾芡。與鮭魚
一樣會溯源產卵，過程艱辛，令人動魄。

我的童年曝曬在蔗葉上
　　曝曬在牛車上
　　曝曬在火車上

風吹過九月的稻埕
我的鄉愁鑲著黃金
　　鑲著南風
　　鑲著太陽

假使童年可以慢慢的咀嚼
一定是香香甜甜的
我咬過的西瓜
仍躺在溪床上睡覺
我划過的竹筏
仍在曾文溪等我出航
我的足跡一直晾在蘆筍園
捨不得回家

聽說胖子阿福在當大老闆
矮仔勝在蓋大樓
愛哭英仔在當幼稚園園長

故鄉是一矸用鄉愁慢慢釀出來的酒
每一口都讓你
醉茫茫

2000/11/27，台南女子技術學院

【附記】海寮屬台南縣安定鄉，是一個靠曾文溪的莊頭，村民
差不多都姓方，種作的農作物主要有西瓜、小玉仔、
蘆筍、稻仔、蕃薯等。莊頭中心有一座廟叫做普陀
寺，主要奉祀楊府太師，後來增加觀音佛祖。海寮是
西港慶安宮的香境（俗稱西港仔香），楊府太師位居
左先鋒，有組南管陣頭參加刈香。

海寮方兇到無人敢惹

這句俗語自小深藏在我心
拔不掉的刺啊
怎會那麼倒楣
我正好住海寮又姓方
左看右看
我都是這麼的溫純又善良
遠看近看
海寮人都這麼的認真又友善
阿公說做人要遵守規矩
阿媽說小孩子要用功讀書
阿爸說做事要腳踏實地
阿母說要與人為善
我都有聽進去
有一天有一個人
尖酸批評海寮人
男的最無情
女的最無義

我氣得揍他一頓
我這才知道海寮方實在有夠兇
我這才知道海寮方實在有夠兇

2001/06/09，台南永康

【附記】海寮位於台南縣安定鄉，為一靠曾文溪的村落，村民
大多姓方。自小常聽外人說起「海寮方兇到無人敢
惹」。起初不知是何意，只知是奚落海寮人很兇惡。
後慢慢得知它的緣由：海寮人兇是因為當被外人欺負
到忍無可忍時，海寮人會全村團結以禦外侮，故給人
很兇的印象。另外，還一句類似的俗諺「海寮方惡甲
無尻川」。

蘇厝

——王船的故鄉

船底的金紙點著
火煙慢慢的升起
火是浪　煙是風
啟航了　啟航了
民眾以虔誠的心
揮別王船
王船在大火中
在煙霧中
緩緩緩緩啟航
揮別王爺
感恩祢代天巡狩庇佑
瘟疫速速離去
COVID-19速速逃亡

祢選擇淳樸的蘇厝
駐蹕
我們用感恩的心

守護王船
我們蓋兩間大廟
奉祀王爺袮
台灣最早的王船祭
從此啟幕

三年一科做醮又到了
敬請王爺上船
曾文溪水青青
王船款款向西出帆
金紙若山高高疊起
王船輕輕向天飛起
瘟疫啊！速速
遠離

2021/10/04，台南永康

與沈光文夜談

我認識汝
在汝過世三百多年後
我們不時在夜晚相約
在我家聚會聊天
汝的眉間結一朵烏雲
「歲歲思歸思不窮」
「夢裡家鄉夜夜還」
我想我可以理解
在目加溜灣西邊的海岸
夜星含著淚珠
汝將鄉愁輕輕的撒在海裡

在2002年的台南
我想買張機票
讓汝飛回
三百多年前
夢中的鄞縣

夢中的兒女
只是　只是
汝會不會像
80、90年代的老榮民
相見不如不見
又飛回來
熟悉的異鄉
台灣

我出生於安定
以前汝教書行醫的地方
我的祖先一定有受到
汝的啟蒙
汝教他們要愛土地愛別人
這也是我們Siraya的優良傳統
汝寫腳踏的風土
這也是我們努力書寫的對象

汝寫了許多鄉愁的詩
我想誰沒有鄉愁呢
汝有故鄉不過沒有國家可回
我有故鄉卻仍無自己的國家
和汝一樣
我的額頭常常結一朵烏雲

2002/09/21，台南永康
九二一台灣地動三週年紀念日

【附記】沈光文（1612-1688），字文開，號斯庵，浙江鄞縣
　　　　（今之寧波）人，南明時代擔任工部郎和太僕少卿。
　　　　鄭成功據守廈門、金門的時候，他本想從金門坐船前
　　　　往泉州，後遇颱風而漂流至台灣。晚年居目加溜灣社
　　　　（今之台南縣善化和安定）教書授徒。在台歷經荷、
　　　　鄭、清三國，他是第一個將漢文化的火種帶來台灣的
　　　　人，並於1685年創立台灣第一個詩社「東吟社」，被
　　　　尊為「海東文獻初祖」、「開台文化祖師」、「台

灣第一士大夫」、「台灣孔子」。著有〈台灣輿圖
考〉、〈草木雜記〉、〈流寓考〉、〈台灣賦〉、
《文開詩文集》，龔顯宗編有《沈光文全集及其研究
資料彙編》（1998，台南：縣立文化中心）。Siraya是
活動於台南、高雄、屏東的平埔族。

公廟[8]

夏日的熱氣，猶停留在廟埕。夜色和熱氣在談判。南海佛祖神明半合的眼睛，像是在入定。香的味道從三百年的香爐飄出來，哦，三百年的香味寫著故鄉的味道、祖先一步一步血汗的足跡。歷代祖先曾在它的四周走過。拜過神明之後，阿祖、阿公、阿媽、阿爸、阿母都曾在這個香爐插過香。在煙霧裊裊的香火中，我看見他們的身影，在廟裡來來去去，笑臉對我說話。

2016/09/11，台南永康

---

[8] 公廟：庄頭廟。此處指台南市安定區海寮的普陀寺。我故鄉的
    公廟。

五分車⁹

聽到「嘟——嘟——」，十歲的童年回來了，甘蔗的童年
回來了。

那年，一枝一枝的甘蔗是阿爸阿母一張一張的鈔票，一張
一張會笑出聲的鈔票。

那年，一枝一枝的甘蔗是我一個一個的夢，一個一個甜甜
的夢。

風吹著甘蔗，甘蔗上歇著一、兩隻烏秋，烏秋的烏是糖廠
的煙囪，煙囪站在火車頭，嘟一聲是糖的童年。

2000/11/19，台南永康

9　五分車：為臺灣糖業鐵路，地方上稱為五分仔車，是為配合臺灣
　　糖業需要而興建的專用鐵路。通常以運送甘蔗、原料為主。

行行復行行

走啊走，走啊走，我一直走一直走。我從我的故鄉台南海寮出發，走到天涯海角。從日出走到日落；從星浮走到星落；從鄉下走到都市；從平原走到深山；從山邊走到海邊；從春天走到夏天；從秋天走到冬天。在雨中走、在風中走、在雪中走。我一直走，一直走，一直走，一直走。要去看這個世界、去聽這個世界、去聞這個世界、去摸這個世界、去嚐這個世界。

2020/01/01，元旦，台南鳳凰山莊

故鄉，載我回歸祖靈的禮車

曾文溪南，春天的番薯將香甜存滿我的心窩，熱天的溪埔
多汁的西瓜和碧綠的蘆筍臥著酣睡，秋天的芒草舞動著白
色的波浪，冬天的蔗園有甜甜的回憶。那是台南縣安定鄉
一個靠曾文溪南岸的小村莊，叫做海寮，是我原始肉體的
紅瓦厝。

兩百年前，海寮就佇立在台江內海邊。三百年前，海寮是
西拉雅族直加弄社捕魚的田園。我好像看見高大的男性祖
先手擤長槍丟射梅花鹿的雄姿，長長的頭髮飛了起來，隨
南風輕輕梳洗，也好像聽見美麗的女性祖先吹著美妙的嘴
琴，琴聲穿過台江內海的波浪星光。故鄉，是載我肉體的
禮車，回歸祖靈。

2005/06/10，台南永康

【二】卿卿如晤

古書走出來的隱者

——致阿公方榮欽（1902-1975）

如咒語，汝嘴裡吟誦著詩句
如密語，汝嘴裡哼著南管樂
在晨曦中，在黃昏中，
汝懷抱著琵琶
如此熟悉又那麼的陌生
汝是從神秘的古書走出來的隱者

晨起，漱洗後
汝慣例散一會兒步
吃過清粥小菜
坐在診間的籐椅上
招喚患者入診間望聞問切
汝是一個為病患把脈的良醫

臨睡前，和汝躺在寢間，
汝慣例清清喉嚨說起兒童故事
虎姑婆的恐怖

林投姐的不幸
是我文學的啟蒙

汝是一個在說故事的慈祥阿公
何時能再聽汝吟哦古詩？
何時能再聽汝彈奏琵琶？
何時能再聽汝說故事？

2021/09/27，台南永康

遙想汝，在相片中

——致阿媽陳笑（1904-1966）

只能在相片中
追尋汝的溫暖和愛
汝過世時我7歲
我竟然對汝沒有半點記憶
只能看看那些年
汝與我的合照

台北新公園裡
我圍著頭巾，汝摟著我
天似乎有點冷，下著微雨
涼亭邊的杜鵑花怒開著
再來是圓山動物園，
我還跟壯碩的大象林旺合照呢
還有那脖子長長的長頸鹿苑春
哦，在野柳
女王成了我們的背景

海浪的聲音似乎
從相片裡溢了出來
就如此
如此而已

或許在南部的家鄉
汝曾帶著我踏遍海寮的稻浪
甘蔗收成時
汝曾削甘蔗解我的渴
也曾在灶肚裡煨著蕃薯
解我的飢
但我竟然
竟然都記不起來

今晚我藉著相片
與汝相會　思念汝

遙想汝
追尋汝的溫暖和愛

2021/11/01，台南永康

濃霧中

——致父親方能安（1925-1982）

我穿過記憶的濃霧
拼圖汝的形象
汝騎著川崎機車
模樣真是帥氣
我坐在機車的油箱上
心情真是昂揚
迎著微風，路樹向後飛逝
看這原野，稻穗鑲著黃金
啊！太陽真是燦爛
啊！空氣真是清新

接下來，是中年的汝
診間充滿著藥水味
桌上的聽筒似乎可以聽見
人間的許多秘密
病人坐在在診間外的長椅上

時鐘滴滴答答訴說著
逐漸褪色的人生
「5號李先生！」
李先生面帶痛苦進到診間
我聽不懂你們的對話
時鐘仍滴滴答答
汝在處方箋上寫了一些字

接下來，是晚年的汝
雙腳腫脹如蒜頭的關節，
汝走的每一條路都是
刀路啊！
每一個微微顫顫的步伐
都是任由刀刃切割
關節裡飽滿的蒜頭
都是白白的石灰粉

半夜的哀鳴
風中的蹙眉
成為我耳裡眼中的風景

那天汝斷氣
在左營海軍總醫院
我推著汝的遺體
走過長長的廊道
夕陽射在汝
黃褐色的臉
消瘦的四肢
是我眼中最後的遺像

至今夢汝汝不來
明天夢中汝會來嗎？

2021/06/26，台南永康

我媽媽是太空人

一九六九年七月二十日
阿姆斯壯
穿著太空衣
揹著氧氣筒
走在月球表面　說出
一句驚天動地的話：
「這雖然是我個人的一小步，
卻是人類的一大步。」
從那時開始，我心裡暗暗的
種下一個夢
夢想做一個太空人

二十八年後
我的夢
沒有發芽
沒有紮根

我媽媽卻成了太空人
也穿太空衣
也揹氧氣筒
月球變成病房
伊連一小步都跨不出去
遑論是一大步

這時我又
種了一個夢
希望媽媽不要做太空人

1997/12/19，台南永康

【附註】我的母親從一九九六年正月初四中風到此時已歷二年
　　　　半，無法坐、無法站、也無法行走，整天躺在病床上。
　　　　她自己無法翻身，也無法自己吃東西和呼吸，需裝上胃
　　　　管和呼吸器。為人子，也只能盡力幫她做復健，請好醫
　　　　生，求上蒼庇佑，希望母親病情儘早康復。

媽媽的皮包

我小的時候
媽媽的皮包是
一只寶箱
有糖果和餅乾
有胭脂也有水粉

我長大後
媽媽的皮包是
一個藥箱
有胃散和萬金油
有高血壓的藥也有救心

此時
媽媽的皮包是
一張病床
裝著她那黑瘦的身軀
也裝著我沉重的心情

1998/07/13，台南永康

媽媽，汝不乖

——致母親方富美（1926-2001）

媽媽，汝不乖
自小汝叫我要乖

「飯要吃多一點
長大好做大事」
「身體要常常運動
手腳敏捷才能走出汝的春天」
「意志要堅強
為汝的光明前程努力」

媽媽，汝不乖
汝　飯只吃一點點
汝　手腳不愛運動
汝　意志也不堅強
我　要和汝一起做大事
我　要和汝一起走出我們的春天
我　要和汝看到我們光明的前程

不過
媽媽，汝不乖

1997/12/04，台南永康

【附註】母親晚年中風，無法自己行動，也無法自己進食。只
　　　　能整天躺在床上。

要去探望母親

若是好天氣
我會去阿里山[1]
看山櫻舞弄春天
不過今天
我要去探望母親

若是下雨天
我會去烏山頭[2]
看雨水吟唱詩歌
不過今天
我要去探望母親

若是艷陽天
我會去鵝鑾鼻[3]

---

[1] 阿里山：台灣一個有名的風景區，以高山火車和森林聞名。
[2] 烏山頭：台灣一個有名的水庫，風景美麗，並可搭船遊湖。
[3] 鵝鑾鼻：台灣一個有名的熱帶海濱度假區，適合游泳、衝浪和

和海浪共舞
不過今天
我要去探望母親

若是下霜雪的冬天
我會躲在家裡
和愛人談情說愛
不過今天
我要去探望母親

此時母親正在住院

1998/05/27，台南永康

浮潛。

春天哪裡去了

最不愛的是陽明山⁴的杜鵑
我最怕看到她豔紅粉白的形影
最不愛的是白河⁵的荷花
我最怕看到她粉妝打扮的容顏
最不愛的是草嶺⁶的菅芒
我最怕看到她舞動秋風的姿勢
最不愛的是楠西⁷的梅花
我最怕看到她無畏霜雪的花蕊

杜鵑有她的春天
荷花有她的夏天

---

⁴　陽明山：台北市近郊的一個國家公園，以杜鵑花和櫻花聞名。
⁵　白河：台南市的一個風景區，以荷花聞名。
⁶　草嶺：雲林縣的一個風景區，以豐富特殊地形景觀聞名。秋天時，山邊水崖長滿芒草，極為美麗。
⁷　楠西：台南市的一個農業區，以出產楊桃和梅子聞名，轄內的梅嶺以梅花最盛名。

菅芒有她的秋天
梅花有她的冬天

媽媽，我問您
您的春天
哪裡去了？

1997/12/15，台南永康

父女的祈禱

小女兒最愛拜拜
每看到寺廟就要拜拜
帶她去中醫院看病
她說要去媽祖廟拜拜
要祈求阿媽的病趕緊好起來

媽祖　媽祖
聽爸爸說
祢最慈悲
祢最疼小孩子
我向祢拜拜
祢要保佑我的阿媽
趕緊好起來
媽祖　媽祖
祢千萬不要忘記

媽祖娘娘
弟子方耀乾
出生於安定
現住永康市
點香來拜拜
一不求名
二不求利
三不求權
只求弟子的母親
安享天年
只求弟子闔家
平安健康

走出廟門
一面回頭一面想
三百多年來

祢一直看顧台灣這個地方
我也祈求祢繼續照顧我們一家人

1998/07/26，台南永康

羊蹄甲如果發燒

羊蹄甲如果發燒
春天就來了
我的心坎裡就會
吟唱著歌詩
我會和伊相對看
看得我倆發燒

羊蹄甲如果發燒
春天就來了
我的心坎裡就會
出太陽
我會和伊坐在樹下
將公園坐到發燒

羊蹄甲如果發燒
春天就來了
我的心坎裡就會

出彩虹
我會牽著伊的手
將馬路踏到發燒

羊蹄甲如果發燒
春天就來了
我的心坎裡就會
開花
我要在每一個人的心裡種花
讓每一個人發燒

1998/03/31，台南女子技術學院

伊在等我

艋舺[8]像箭
射過金色的相思海
風的翅膀像伊的嘴唇
親吻著我的臉
矯捷的麻虱目[9]
在金色的水裡競跑
伊說麻虱目是愛情的符咒
一定要載一船回去
今晚在竹林下和伊
配著月光享用

我一定要載一船回去
伊一定在岸邊
夕陽點亮伊的眼眸

---

[8] 艋舺（bangka）：船，平埔族西拉雅語。
[9] 麻虱目：虱目魚。古早台江內海出產虱目魚，目前仍是台南、高
雄地區的名產。

如兩朵熱情的火花
等我

我一定要載一船回去
伊一定在岸邊
Cocoa的皮膚金亮滑嫩
飽滿的胸前開兩朵圓仔花
等我

我一定要載一船回去
今晚和伊
溶成月光
在竹林樹下

2005/09/03，台南永康

歌

——致牽手Demi

用我最深情的眼睛
將汝看作一幅油畫

用我最靈敏的耳朵
將汝聽作一首小夜曲

用我最認真的鼻子
將汝嗅成一瓶香水

用我最熱情的嘴唇
將汝吻成一束玫瑰花

用我最溫柔的雙手
將汝塑作一尊琉璃

最後
用我最讚嘆的心

將汝讀成一棵楊柳
和一棵榕樹

1995/03/29，華語初稿
1998，台語定稿，台南永康

三十一年後的掌聲

——予牽手Demi

那年汝的模樣
我想我仍然記得
汝十一歲
我也十一歲
我們同班　南安國小五年忠班
初次見面　應該是在九月

汝不高大
瘦瘦的一個小女孩
頭髮留到耳邊
赤腳　細細的腿
靜靜的　有兩朵倔強的
眼睛

汝書讀得很好
常常一枝鉛筆寫到
剩一小節

握在細細的手裡
努力的犁作業簿

家裡沒故事書可看
學校圖書室的書
都讓汝借光光
〈賣火柴的小女孩〉
常在颱風下雨的夜晚
讓汝想起還有媽媽的溫暖

後來聽說
畢業那一年
汝是全校第一名
不能上台領最高的獎
縣長獎是要給那個
老師的兒子

畢業典禮那一天
不曾穿過鞋的汝
細細的腳丫子
穿一雙向阿媽借的鞋子
太大一雙鞋
上台領第二獎
一步　嘆
　　　一步　嘆
　　　　　一步　嘆
　　　　　　　一步　嘆
走上台上
那時木麻黃皆挺立靜默
蟬在校園裡大聲抗議

2002/10/14，台南永康

汝的眉間結一朵憂愁

今晚汝又比我早睡
沒跟我道：晚安
我斜躺在汝的身邊
看我主編　才出版的
《台語文學讀本》
轉頭看汝
烏溜溜的長髮披在枕頭上
將嫩白透亮的臉環抱著
我曾輕輕捏過的鼻仔
緩緩的呼吸人間歲月
我曾親吻過的嘴唇無辜
靜默無語
兩隻雙眼皮的大眼睛這時閉著
眼睫毛溫柔的看顧一夜的眠夢
這個臉嫁我20年
在我的心目中
一直是一個美麗的陶瓷

這時眉頭間結一朵憂愁

我將書放置胸前
溫柔的燈光
將我的手剪成一個影子
我想要抹平妳的眉間
可是憂愁馬上又糾結起來
我的手摸過汝的
額頭
　　眉毛
　　　　鬢角
　　　　　　臉頰

在溫暖恬靜的床上
我思考憂愁的哲學
是不是上班太累
是不是身體不舒服

是不是煩惱女兒們
抑是我愛汝的電不夠

二十年前
汝將汝交給我
我暗暗對自己說
不讓黑暗靠近汝
很顯然　我失約了
胸前的《台語文學讀本》滑落床下
我躺落床將汝的手牽著
汝眉間的憂愁
一直蔓延
　　　一直蔓延
蔓延到我的眉間

2003/02/22，台南永康永二街

南方的鳳凰花，向前行

——致女兒涵

抱著祝福的心情
要為汝的希望加分
雖然武林高手全到
要站穩
心頭定
有信心就會贏

台北擺一個
冷冷的嘴臉
宛然武林高手
冷冷的心胸
台大陽明論劍
無須必死的決心
但要有奮戰的精神
汝是南方熱情的鳳凰花
輸贏都要愛堅強面對

牽著汝的手
走在台北街頭
就像過去十七年來
我熱滾滾的手要給汝信心
燃燒吧
我勇健的手要給汝意志
堅強吧
要帶汝上戰場
只有經火煉才會變成金
只有經焠煉才會變成鋼
南方的鳳凰花
汝自去
向前行
爸爸永遠支持汝

2000/03/26，寫在台北回台南的莒光號火車內

【附記】陪大女兒上台北參加台大（3/24-3/25）、陽明（3/26）醫學系申請入學考試，有感而寫。現將這首詩打入電腦的時候，已經知曉她已考上陽明醫學系了。

女兒的「國語」考卷

——致女兒萱

女兒一面跑一面哭回來
老師罵她胡亂寫
考試卷上面一顆大鴨蛋

造句：
1.……有時……有時……
答：我們老師有時會罵人，有時會打人。
2.……中秋……
答：一年四季當中秋天最美麗。
3.……會……不會……
答：我爸爸說：總統　蔣公會大便，不會講台語。
4.一朵朵……
答：一朵朵的綿羊在天空游泳。
5.……綠油油……
答：春天把草原綠油油了。

是哪裡錯了，女兒問我
因為汝是詩人，我回答

1999/01/21，台南永康

英語篇

My Hometown Shines in My Heart: Preface "The Golden Zengwen River"

Yaw-chien Fang

"The Golden Zengwen River"（金色的曾文溪）is a trilingual collection of poems, written in Taiwanese, Mandarin, and English. The poems focus on my family and my hometown, Anding Township（安定）. The collection is divided into two series: (1) Golden Hometown, (2) My Beloved.

The first section contains poems about my hometown. I was born, raised, and educated in Hailiao. Anding, Tainan. I attended Nanan Elementary School, and Anding Junior High School. My hometown nurtured me through my youth. Anding is an agricultural town on the banks of the meandering Zengwen River. The river forms the northern border of the town, and the western and southern districts are connected to old Tainan City. Shanhua is our neighbor to the east and beyond that lies the beautiful and verdant Central Mountain Range.

Anding was originally a part of the old land of the Tackalan (Tackalan). The Tackalan are a people group affiliated with the Backloun of the Siraya tribe of the Pingpu ethnic group. From our past geographical environment and relics, we understand the current name of the village, such as Gangkou, Gangnan, Gangzaiwei, Hailiao, Duzaitou, Dingzhouzai, Xiazhouzai, Zhonglunzai, Shalun and so on.

The river Zengwen often flooded, and frequently diverted its course; causing large amounts of sediment to gradually fill the inland sea of the Taijiang Inland Sea, which eventually became dry land. As a result, the port lost its function, and the region became a rural area. Many of the current residents of the area make a living through agriculture. In addition to growing rice and sweet potatoes, Anding is known for producing watermelon, sesame, and asparagus. Other than the newly established TSMC 18 plant in the recently stable northwest corner of the region, there are few major companies in the area. The current ethnic structure comprises mainly Taiwanese people-simple folk who practice simple customs. The nostalgic poems in this book are dedicated to my hometown. With these poems, my memories of Anding are kept alive in my heart.

The second section draws on my life with my family. My family originated in Tong'an, Quanzhou, Fujian. We moved across the Taiwan

Strait and settled into the immigrant life during the Qianlong period of the Qing Empire in the 18th century. Three centuries later, we are no longer immigrants, and the foreign land has become our new hometown and a new paradise. Our home is known as Hailiao because it is situated by the sea. For generations my ancestors worked hard, fought drought and famine. My grandfather, Ingkhim Png, is a member of the sixth generation of the Fang family who was born and raised in Taiwan. This collection of poems describes the life and memories of the sixth, seventh, eighth and ninth generation families. The poems are inhabited by my family members: some of the characters are my grandfather Ingkhim Png（方榮欽）, my grandmother Tshio Tan（陳笑）, my father Lingan Png（方能安）, my mother Hubi Png（方富美）, my wife Kimtiu Te（戴錦綢）, my eldest daughter Ingham（方穎涵）, and my youngest daughter Ingsuan（方穎萱）. These poems are memories of my family. They express my love and emotions for my family, and our legacy for future generations. Therefore, my voice expresses warmth and nostalgia for the past.

I would like to thank the poet Kuei-shien Lee for facilitating the publishing of this book of poems. I also want to thank my outstanding student, Dr. Chuen-shin Tai, for translating the poems into English. I would also like to thank Dr. Jon Nichols for his help with English revision. They are both currently Assistant Professors in the Applied English Department of Shih Chien University.

--2021.12.18, 63rd birthday.

CONTENTS

Part One:
Golden Hometown

Golden Zengwen River

The golden dusk lies on the glided Zengwen River

Omar Khayyam[1] draws forth a song - gently

Slight tipsy

Sandro Botticelli's[2] *Primavera*

Unveiled on a bamboo raft.

Demi's hair streams toward the west

Like a phoenix.

In her eyes

I smile like a golden red paulownia flower.

At this moment, the sugar cane train

Carries the sweetness of hope

---

[1] Omar Khayyam (?-1123): Born in Naxa Fort, the capital of the Persian province of Gaulassen, one of the wisest men of his time, author of Rubáiyát (meaning "quatrain").

[2] Sandro Botticelli (1445-1510): Italian Renaissance painter, best known for his painting "The Birth of Venus", considered to be the epitome of the spirit of the Renaissance. "Primavera (Spring)" is full of joy.

From the Sigang Bridge.

As purple thistle flowers[3] grow

On both sides of the river.

The yellow Chinese lxeris flowers wave

And send greetings.

The gold stream

Flows quietly westward

We wait for dusk

When the sky fades in pale sunset

And stars appear in the dark night

They scintillate and shimmer.

-- Yongkang, Tainan, 2001/06/07

---

[3]   Purple thistle flower: the purple thistle. In early spring, purple flowers bloom in the fields.

Chinese lxeris also known as Rabbit Milk Weed. It is a perennial herb, Asteraceae, with golden flowers in spring.

【Notes】Zengwen River is the most important stream in the Jianan Plain, which flows through Hailiao in Anding District and Sigang District in Tainan City. Views from the bridge are the most beautiful in this area. During the past, whenever the sun slanted westward, people often stayed on the bridge to see the entire view of the sunset. A small sugar factory railway would run on the bridge. During winter, I often watch the sugar cane train transporting sugarcane passing by the bridge. The sugar industry has fallen, and the railway has been demolished. The riverside where Demi and I had walked is still there, and the vehicles on the Sigang Bridge are busy as usual. However, the sugar cane train on the bridge, the paulownia flowers by the stream, the purple flower thistle, and the Chinese lxeris are only seen in the spring breeze kept in my sweet memories.

Golden Hometown Anding

My golden hometown Anding

Such beauty.

Blue skies and white clouds

The sweet breath and vivid colors of vast panoramas of flowers

The scenery radiant in colors.

My gold hometown Anding

Rich in commodities.

Gathering asparagus in spring and gleaning watermelons in summer.

Reaping rice in autumn and harvesting sesame in winter.

God is kind and merciful.

My golden hometown Anding

I venerate you

As the river envelops the north, like a mother's embrace.

The rice fields are radiant gold, like the warmth of a father's love

Evoking passionate, intoxicated love.

Dew in the morning of Anding
Scattered with crystalline pearls.
The evening sun shines on the Zengwen River
Painting a winding golden tapestry.

My hometown
You are my mother,
I honor you
My hometown
You are my father,
I offer my gratitude.

Yongkang, Tainan, 2021/10/01

Hailiao: Hometown Nostalgia

I plucked the setting sun and
Attached it to the temple roof.
A quarter century of memories hidden within a box———
illuminated.
The Buddha's eyebrow shakes the past awake
Stirring my stranded childhood
Rowing the boat gently.

Years migrate like whitebait.
Dad raises his hoe – invincible.
Mother's hands are carved with the wind and frost - a banyan tree.
That year, at the festival, sounds of temple drums proclaimed
Who the winners of the Taiwanese puppet show and Taiwanese
opera competition are?

The wind blows in the sugar cane field in December.
My childhood sunbathed on cane leaves

Revealed on the ox cart
Displayed on the train.

The wind blows rice field in September.
My yearning for home is studded in gold
                    Bordered by the south wind
                    Enwrought by the sun.

If I can chew and taste my childhood
It is candy-coated.
Just like the honeyed watermelon
Which sleeps on the creek bed.
On the bamboo raft I row
It waits for me to sail down Zengwen River.
Reluctant to go home,
I leave my footprints in the asparagus garden.
I heard that Afuzai is now a big boss

And the once short kid Shengzai is building high towers
And Yingzai the once crying baby, is now the kindergarten principal.

Hometown is a wine haltingly brewed in nostalgia.
Each sip makes you
woozy.

Tainan Women's College of Arts and Technology, 2000/11/27

Hailiao Fangs Are so Fierce that No One Dares to Provoke Them

Since I was young there has been a question in my heart.

It's like an unplucked thorn.

Why do I have such bad luck?

I happen to live in Hailiao———my family name is Fang

I look to the left and right.

I am gentle and kind.

I look far away and close within.

Hailiao people are earnest and wholehearted

Grandpa says we must obey the rules.

Grandma tells us to be diligent.

Dads asks us to have our feet on the ground.

Mom wants us to be kind.

I listen to them.

One day a person

said some harsh things about Hailio people:

The men are ruthless.

The women are heartless.

In a rage, I beat him up.

This is when I understood; Hailio people are fierce.

This is when I understood; Hailio people are fierce.

Yongkang, Tainan, 2001/06/09

【Note】 Hailiao is located in Anding Township, Tainan and a village near Zengwen River. Most villagers have the surname Fang. Since childhood I hear from outsiders, "Hailiao is untamed that no one dares to provoke them." At first, I didn't know what it meant, but I only knew that Hailiao people are vicious. Later on, I learned the reason: Hailiao people are ferocious because when they are bullied by outsiders, Hailiao people will unite in the village to guard against outside insults, which leaves people a very bold impression.

Sucuo: A Hometown of the King Ship

The gold paper at the bottom of the boat is ignited.

The smoke slowly rises,

The fire is the waves, the smoke is the wind.

The vessel sets sail.

People with a pious heart

Say farewell to the king ship.

The king ship is on fire——burning,

Smoldering.

They say goodbye and

Bid farewell to the kings.

They thank the guardians

And pray that the plague leaves rapidly.

They pray that Covid 19 flees speedily.

You chose Sucuo, a small village

As stopover place during your journey.

We are grateful

金色的曾文溪
The Golden Zengwen River

That the ship defends us.
We built two vast temples to
Worship the god-princes.
The earliest royal ship festival
Started here.

The Festival have come once every 3 years.
We ask the god-princes to come aboard.
The Zengwen River is green.
The king-ship sails westward
The gold paper is stacked high
The king-ship flies gently to the sky
The plague!
Scoot away!

Yongkang, Tainan, 2021/10/04

Night Talks with Shen Guang-wen

I know you

Even though you died 300 years ago.

From time to time, we meet during the night

To chat in my home.

A dark cloud lies between your brows

"From the long years of yearning,

I dreaming of my hometown."

I empathize.

On the west coast of Bakaloan,

The starry night is full of teardrops.

You gently spread homesickness into the sea.

In Tainan 2002

I would like to buy you a ticket

To fly back to your hometown,

Yin county you dream about,

The children you dream about,

Three hundred years ago.

It is just that

Will you be like a

Veteran from the 80s or 90s

Who would rather not meet hometown again

Flying back

To the familiar foreign land

Taiwan.

I was born in Anding

Where you used to teach and practice medicine.

My ancestors must have perceived

Your enlightenment.

You taught them to love the land and others.

This is also the fine tradition of our Siraya.

You write your footprints left in the interior.

We write about the same things.

Your poems are Nostalgic.

Aren't we all homesick?

You have a hometown but without a country to return to.

I have a hometown, still not a country.

Same as you.

I also have dark clouds on my forehead.

Yongkang, Tainan, 2002/09/21
921 Taiwan Earthquake 3rd Anniversary

【Note】 Shen Guang-wen (1612-1688), courtesy name Wen-kai, was born in Yinxian County, Zhejiang Province (now Ningbo), and served as Gongbu Lang and Taipu Shaoqing in the Nanming period. When Koxinga was guarding Xiamen and Kinmen, he originally wanted to take a boat from Kinmen to Quanzhou, but then drifted to Taiwan during a typhoon. In his later years, Bakaloan (now Shanhua and Anding, Tainan County) he became a teacher. He was the first to bring the flames of Han culture to Taiwan through the Netherlands, Zheng, and Qing. In 1685, he founded the first poetry society "Dongyin Society" in Taiwan, and was honored as "The First Haidong Literature". "Ancestor", "The Founding Master of Taiwan Culture", "Taiwan's First Scholar Official", "Taiwan Confucius". He is the Author of "Taiwan Maps", "Grass and Trees Miscellaneous Notes", "Liu Yu Kao", "Taiwan Fu", "Wen Kai Poems and Essays", Gong Xianzong compiled "Shen Guangwen Collection and Research Materials Collection" (1998, Tainan: County Cultural Center). Siraya is a Pingpu ethnic group living in Tainan, Kaohsiung, and Pingtung.

Temple

The heat of summer still dwells in the temple. Night and heat are negotiating. The half-closed eyes of the Nanhai Buddha are mediating. The smell of incense wafted from the 300-year-old incense burner. Oh, the smell of the 300-year-old emblems the taste of hometown and the footprints of the ancestors' blood and sweat. Ancient ancestors have walked through here. After worshiping the gods, Great Grandma, Grandpa, Grandma, Dad, and Mom all put incense in this censer. In the smoky incense, I see their figures and faces, coming and going in the temple; they smile and talk to me.

Yongkang, Tainan, 2016/09/11

【Note】 The temple here refers to Putuo Temple in Hailiao, Anding District, Tainan City, my hometown.

The Sugar Cane Train

Hearing the sound of "woo-woo", brings childhood memories sugarcane and being ten.

That year, the stalks of sugarcane were banknotes for Mom and Dad, and the banknotes laughed out loud.

That year, the stalks of sugarcane inhabited my dreams, sweet dreams one after another.

The wind blows the sugarcane, and one or two black crows rest in their midst. Their raven hue indistinguishable from the sugar factory chimney. Indistinguishable from the locomotive's funnel. When I hear the train's whistle, I remember my sugarcane childhood.

Yongkang, Tainan, 2000/11/19

【Note】 Sugarcane train: It is the Taiwan Sugar Industry Railway, known locally as the Wufen Train. It is a special railway built to meet the needs of the Taiwan sugar industry. It mainly transports sugar cane.

Walking and Going

Walk and go, walk and go, I keep walking. I set off from my hometown of Hailiao, Tainan and walk to the ends of the world. From sunrise to sunset; from star rise to star set; from country to city; from the plains to the deep mountains; from mountain to sea; from spring to summer; from autumn to winter. I walk in the rain, walk in the wind, walk in the snow. I keep walking, keep going, keep carrying, keep marching. To see this world, to hear this world, to savor this world, to touch this world, to taste this world.

New Year's Day, Tainan Phoenix Resort, 2020/01/01

Hometown, The Hearse that Takes Me Back to My Ancestors

In spring sweet potatoes grow on the banks of the Zenwen River. On hot summer days, juicy watermelon and green asparagus lay sleepily on the river land. In autumn the awn grass dances in white waves, and the sugarcane garden has sweet winter-time memories. Hailiao is a small village on the south bank of Zengwen River in Anding Township, Tainan County. It is the red tile house of my primitive flesh.

Two hundred years ago, Hailiao stood on the coast of the Tai Jiang Inner Sea. Three hundred years ago, Hailiao was the farmland where the Siraya tribe Tackalan people lived. I see the tall male ancestor hurling a long spear at a majestic sika deer. His long hair is flying, gently groomed by the South Wind. I hear a graceful female ancestor playing the beautiful harp. The sounds permeate the waves and starlight of the Tai Jiang Inner Sea. My hometown is a hearse returning my body to the ancestral spirit.

Yongkang, Tainan, 2005/06/10

Part Two:
My Beloved

The Hermit Who Came Out of the Ancient Book: To Grandpa Png Ing-khim (1902-1975)

Like a mantra, you are chanting verses

Like a whisper, the Nanguan humming in your mouth.

In the dawn, in the dusk

You hold the lute in your arms.

It is familiar yet foreign

You are the Hermit who came out of the ancient book.

You would freshen up after waking up.

You used to take a short walk.

You have rice gruel and side dishes.

Sitting on the wicker chair in the clinic office

Calling patients into the office to look, listen, ask questions and feel their pulse.

You are a good doctor who takes good care of patients.

Before sleep, you sat by my bed

You clear your throat and tell fairy tales.

The horror of Aunt Tiger

And the misfortune of Sister Na-tau,

Were the stories that inspired my love for literature.

You are a loving grandpa who tells me stories.

When can I listen to your ancient poems again?

When can I listen to your lute playing again?

When can I listen to your story telling again?

Yongkang, Tainan, 2021/09/07

Missing You Through the Photos: To Grandma Tan Tshio (1904-1966)

Only in the photos,

I search for the warmth and love from you.

I was 7 years-old when you passed away.

Alas! I have no any memories of you at all.

Only can I see those

Photos of you and me.

In Taipei New Park

I was wearing a headscarf, and you hugged me.

It seemed to be a little cold and raining,

The Rhododendrons by the gazebo were in full bloom.

Next photo is Yuan-shan Zoo.

I even took a photo with the sturdy elephant Lin-wang.

And the long neck giraffe Yuanchun.

Oh, it's in Yehliu.

The queen became our background.

The sound of the waves seems to

Overflow from the photo.

That's it.

That's all!

Perhap in the hometown of the south

You once took me across the rice waves of Hailiao.

When the sugar cane was harvested,

You cut the sugar cane to quench my thirst.

You also simmered sweet potatoes in the stove

To relieve my hunger.

But I couldn't

Even remember.

Tonight through the photos,

I see you, miss you,

Think of you,

Searching warmth and love from you.

Yongkang, Tainan, 2021/11/01

The Thick Fog: To My Father Png Ling-an (1925-1982)

I pass through the fog of memory,

Your image is a jigsaw.

You ride a Kawasaki motorcycle,

Looking so handsome.

I sit on the fuel tank,

Feeling so uplifted.

I facing the breeze, the trees by the road fly backwards.

I looking towards the field, the grains of rice are studded with gold.

Ah! The sun is so shining.

Ah! The air is so freshening.

Then, you are middle-aged.

The clinic smells like medicine.

The stethoscope can hear

The secrets of the people.

The patients are on the bench outside

And the clock ticking the story

Of life fading.

Mr. Lee No.5!

Mr. Li came to the clinic with pain.

I don't understand your conversation.

The clock continues to tick

And you write a prescription.

Eventually, you are old.

Your feet swollen like garlic joints.

Every step you take is

Like walking on razors.

Every trembling step is

Like the cut of a blade.

Cloves of garlic in your knuckles

Are white like powder.

Your wail in the middle of the night,

Your frown in the wind,

Are the scenery in my ears.

The day you passed away

At Zuoying Naval hospital,

I pushed your body down

The long corridor.

The sunset on your

Tawny face

And your thin limbs

Is the last portrait in my eyes.

You haven't been in my dreams before

Will you be in my dream tomorrow?

Yongkang, Tainan, 2021/06/26

My Mother Is an Astronaut

July 20th, 1969

Armstrong

Wore a space suit

With an oxygen tank

When he walked on the surface of the moon.

He said stunning words to the world:

"That's one small step for man,

One giant leap for mankind."

At that moment, I secretly

Planted a dream

To become an astronaut.

Twenty-eight years later,

My dream

Hasn't sprouted,

Hasn't taken root.

However, my mom has become an astronaut.

She wears a spacesuit
That carries an oxygen tank.
The moon is now a hospital ward.
She can't even take a small step
Not to mention a giant leap.

Now
I have a new dream.
I don't want my mother to be an astronaut.

Yongkang, Tainan, 1997/12/01

【Note】 It has been two and a half years since my mother suffered a stroke on the fourth day of the first lunar month in 1996. She cannot sit, stand, or walk. She is in a hospital bed all day. She can't turn over by herself, and can't eat or breathe on her own, so she must be fed with a stomach tube and respirator. As her son, I do my best to help her recover, seeking the best doctors, asking God to bless her, and holding on to faith I hope that my mother will recover.

Mother's Purse

When I was young,

Mom's purse was

A treasure chest.

It contained candies and cookies.

It also had rouge and gouache.

As I grew up

Mom's purse became

A medicine box.

It had stomach medicine and Tiger Balm oil.

It also had high blood medicine that could save her life.

Now

Mom's purse is

A hospital bed.

The bed she lies on holds her dark weak body.

It also holds my heavy sad heart.

Yongkang, Tainan, 1998/07/13

Mom, You Are Mischievous: To My Mother Png Hu-bi (1926-2001)

Mom, you are mischievous.

You told me to be a good child when I was young.

"You need to eat more,

So you can do great things when you grow up."

"You need to exercise often,

So you can increase your speed and agility."

"You need to have strong will,

So you can obtain a bright and successful future."

Mom you are mischievous.

You don't eat much.

You don't exercise.

You are not strong.

I want to accomplish great things with you.

I want to walk the path of achievements with you.

I want to see a better tomorrow with you.

But

Mom, you are mischievous.

Yongkang, Tainan, 1997/12/04

【Note】 My mother suffered from a stroke in her late years and was unable to eat or move on her own, now she can only lay on her bed all day.

Visiting Mom

If the weather is nice,
I will go to Alishan[1]
To see the cherry dance in the mountain during spring.
But today,
I will visit my mom.

If it rains,
I will go to Wushantou[2]
To hear the rain sing
But today,
I will visit my mom.

---

[1] Alishan: A famous scenic spot in Taiwan, famous for its alpine trains and forests.
[2] Wushantou: A well-known reservoir in Taiwan, with beautiful scenery, and boat tours.

If it's sunny

I will go to Eluanbi[3]

To dance with the waves.

But today,

I will visit my mom.

If it's frosty winter

I will hide at home

And be with my lover

But today,

I will visit my mom.

Now, my mom is the hospital.

Yongkang, Tainan, 1998/05/27

---

[3] Eluanbi: A famous tropical seaside resort in Taiwan, for swimming, surfing and snorkeling.

Where is Spring?

Rhododendrons aren't my favorites at Yangmingshan.[4]

I am afraid of their bright red and white figures.

I dislike the lotus at Baihe.[5]

I dread seeing her wearing makeup.

I loathe the silver grass at Caoling.[6]

It frightens me to see her dancing in the autumn breeze.

I don't like to see the plums in Nanxi[7]

It horrifies me to see how fearless of the frost she is.

---

[4] Yangmingshan: A national park on the outskirts of Taipei City, famous for its rhododendrons and cherry blossoms.

[5] Baihe: A scenic area in Tainan City, famous for Lotus.

[6] Caoling: A scenic spot in Yunlin County, famous for its rich special topographical landscapes. In autumn, the mountainside water cliffs are covered with beautiful Miscanthus.

[7] Nanxi: An agricultural area in Tainan City, famous for producing carambola and plums, and Meiling is most famous for its plum blossoms.

金色的曾文溪
The Golden Zengwen River

The Rhododendron has her spring.

The Lotus has her summer.

The Silver grass has her autumn.

The Plum has her winter.

Mom, may I ask

about your spring?

Where has it gone?

--Yongkang, Tainan, 1997/12/15

Father and Daughter's Pray

My little daughter loves to worship at the temple.

She worships at every temple she sees.

I take her to the Chinese medicine hospital.

She says she wants to go to worship at Mazu temple,

So she can pray that grandma has a speedy recovery.

Mazu, Mazu,

My father tells me

you are merciful.

You love children

So I pray to you

To bless my grandma

So that she will recover from sickness.

Mazu, Mazu,

You must not forget my prayers.

Mazu goddess

金色的曾文溪

The Golden Zengwen River

I am your disciple Png Yawchien.

I was born in Anding

And live in Yongkang City.

I light incense,

Not for fame,

Not for profit,

Not for power.

I pray that my mom

Will have a happy life in old age.

I pray that my family

Will have good health and happiness.

Stepping out of the temple,

I look back and think.

That for over three hundred years,

you have been blessing Taiwan.

I pray that you will continue to bless all those I love.

Yongkang, Tainan, 1998/07/26

If the Orchid Tree Has a Fever

If the orchid tree has a fever,

Then spring is here.

In my heart,

I will sing.

I will look at her

And see the red fever shyness on her face.

If the orchid tree has a fever,

Then spring is here.

In my heart,

There will be sunshine.

She and I will sit under the tree

Until the bench is hot like a fever.

If the orchid tree has a fever,

Then spring is here.

In my heart,

It will grow a rainbow.

I will hold her hand

And walk until our feet are burning hot.

If the orchid tree has a fever,

Then spring is here.

In my heart,

Flowers will bloom.

I want to plant a flower in everyone's heart

So that everyone can feel the fever in their heart.

Tainan Women's College of Arts and Technology, 1998/03/31

She Is Waiting for Me

Bangka[8] is like an arrow,

Shooting through the golden sea of lovesickness.

The wings of wind are like your lips,

Kissing my face.

The brisk milkfish

Are racing in the water.

She says the milkfish can cast love spells.

I must bring back a boatload of them.

Tonight under the bamboo forest

We enjoy it under the moonlight.

I will bring back a boatload of milkfish.[9]

She will be at the shore.

The setting sun lights up her eyes

---

[8]   Bangka: meaning boat, in Siraya language of Pingpu people.

[9]   Milkfish was bred in the Taijiang Inland Sea in past times, and it is still a popular product in Tainan and Kaohsiung.

Like two passionate sparking flowers,

Waiting for me.

I will bring back a boatload of milkfish.

She will be at the shore.

Cocoa skin golden and smooth

Just like the blooming flowers on her chest

Waiting for me.

I will bring back a boatload of milkfish.

Tonight she and I

Both melted into the moonlight

Under the bamboo trees.

Yongkang, Tainan, 2005/09/03

Song: For My Beloved Wife Demi

With my most affectionate eyes,
I picture you as an oil painting.

Using my sensitive ears,
I hear you as a serenade.

Using my nose,
I sniff you like a bottle of perfume.

Using my passionate lips,
I kiss you like a bouquet of roses.

Using my gentle hands,
I sculpt you into the shape of a glass.

Then
With my most admired heart,

I read you as a willow

And a banyan tree.

First draft in Mandarin, 1995/03/29
Finalized in Taiwanese, Yongkang, Tainan, 1998

Applause from Thirty-one Years Later: For My Love Demi

The way you looked that year,

I still remember.

You were eleven years old

And I was also eleven years old.

We were in the same fifth-year loyalty class at Nanan Elementary School.

We first met in September.

You were not tall.

You were just a skinny little girl,

With ear-length hair,

bare feet and thin legs.

Quietly, you showed your two stubborn

eyes.

You made good grades.

You always used the same pencil until only

A little piece was left.

Holding the pencil with your thin hand

Working hard in the workbook.

There were no story books at home for you to read.

You borrowed all the books

In the school library.

On windy and rainy nights

"The Little Match Girl"

Reminds you of your mother's warmth.

Later I heard that

You were the top student in our whole school

—the year we graduated.

You weren't presented the award on the stage.

The County Governor's award was given to

To the teacher's son.

On graduation day

You who never worn shoes

Thin feet

wore a pair of shoes that was borrowed from grandma.

The shoes were too big.

You were rewarded second prize on stage.

A step, tap

     A step, tap

          A step, tap

               A step, tap

Walking onto the stage.

The casuarina stood upright and quietly,

But the cicada protested loudly making a fuss at school.

Yongkang, Tainan, 2002/10/14

A Flower Called Sorrow Grew Between Your Eyebrows

Tonight you fell asleep earlier than me.

You didn't say Goodnight.

I reclined by your side,

Reading my editor-in-chief and just published

"Taiwanese Literature Reader."

Turning my head and looking at you,

I see your long slick and dark hair on the pillow,

Embracing your soft and fair-skinned face.

The nose I have pinched gently,

breathing through life and time slowly.

The lips I have kissed are innocent

And silent.

Your two big eyes with double eyelids are now closed.

Your eyelashes tenderly asleep.

Your face married to me for twenty years.

In my heart,

You have always been a beautiful piece of pottery.

However, a flower known as sorrow grows between your eyebrows.

I lay the book on my chest.

The gentle light

Shapes my hand into a shadow.

I want to smooth the sorrow from your eyebrows,

But the sorrow soon became entangled again.

My hand touches your

Forehead,

    Eyebrows,

        Temple,

            cheek.

On the warm and peaceful bed,

I think about the philosophy of sadness.

Are you tired from work?

Are you sick?

Are you worried about our daughters?

Or is it because I do not love you enough?

Twenty years ago

You give yourself to me.

I secretly told myself

To never let darkness come near you.

Apparently, I didn't keep my promise.

"Taiwanese literature Reader" slips from my chest and falls under the

bed.

I lay down on the bed and hold your hand.

Your eyebrows are full of sorrow.

It keeps growing

      keeps growing

growing until it is between my eyebrows.

Yong 2nd St., Yongkang, Tainan, 2003/02/22

The Phoenix Flower from the South, Moving Forward: For Ham

Being in a blissful mood,

I wish you the best.

Although there are other top martial arts masters,

You stand firm,

You keep calm.

If you have confidence, you will win.

Taipei shows

A Cold face.

Just like a master of martial arts

With a cold heart.

At the National Taiwan University and Yangming tournament

You don't need to fight to the death.

But you must have a strong fighting will.

You are the passionate Phoenix Flower from the south

Strong enough to take victory or defeat.

Holding your hand

As we walk the streets of Taipei

Just like we have for the past seventeen years

My hot hand gives you confidence

To burn.

My strong hand will give you the will and power.

Be strong.

You are on the battlefield.

Gold must be refined by fire;

Steel can only be formed quenching.

You are the Phoenix Flower from the south.

You do go by yourself,

Walking forward.

Dad is always here to support you.

Written on the Chu-Kuang Express from Taipei towards Tainan, 2000/03/26

【Note】 I wrote this poem when accompanying my eldest daughter to Taipei to take the entrance examination for the Department of Medicine of National Taiwan University (3/24-3/25) and Yangming University (3/26). When I wrote this poem on my computer, I already knew that she had been admitted to the Department of Medicine, Yangming University.

My Daughter's "Mandarin" Exam Paper: For Suan

My daughter cried as she ran home

After her teacher had scolded her for writing nonsense.

There was a huge zero scored on the exam paper.

Sentence-making:

1.······Sometimes······Sometimes

Answer: Sometimes our teacher will scold us, sometimes our teacher

will punish us.

2.······Mid-Autumn······

Answer: Mid-Autumn is the most beautiful season of the year.

3.······can······cannot······

Answer: My dad said: President Chiang Kai-shek can poop, but

cannot speak Taiwanese.

4. ······a bunch of······

Answer: A bunch of sheep is swimming on the sky.

5.······Green······

Answer: Spring greens the grassland.

My daughter asked me what mistake she had made.

I replied, you was a poet.

Yongkang, Tainan, 1999/01/21

金色的曾文溪
The Golden Zengwen River

作者簡介

　　方耀乾（1958-），成功大學台灣文學博士。現任臺中教育大學臺語系特聘教授、本土語文（閩、客、原）課綱研修委員兼總召集人、台灣文學學會理事、World Union of Poets總顧問兼台灣區會長、World Nation Writers' Union台灣首席代表等。詩集有《阮阿母是太空人》、《烏／白》、《台窩灣擺擺》等13冊。論著專書有《對邊緣到多元中心：台語文學的主體建構》、《台灣母語文學：少數文學史書寫理論》等6冊。曾獲「Pentasi B.終身成就貢獻獎」（印度）、「Mewadev國際文學偶像桂冠獎」（印度）、世界人民作家協會頒發「全球之光獎」（哈薩克）、世界文學交流貢獻獎（蒙古國）、台江文化貢獻獎（第32屆世界詩人大會）、巫永福文學評論獎、榮後台灣詩人獎、吳濁流文學獎新詩正獎等。詩被翻譯成英文、日文、西班牙文、土耳其文、蒙古文、孟加拉文、俄文、羅馬尼亞文、尼泊爾文發表。

Yaw-chien Fang (born in 1958, Tainan, Taiwan) is a leading poet, writer, scholar, and editor in Taiwan. He obtained his Ph.D. degree in Taiwanese literature, National Cheng-kung University. Currently he is Distinguished Professor of Department of Taiwanese Languages & Literature, National Taichung University of Education. He has been the presidents, publishers, editors-in-chief of several important associations and magazines. His poetry has been translated into English, Spanish, Chinese, Japanese, Turkish, Mongolian, Bengali, Telugu, Romanian, etc., and has been read in International Poetry Recitals in many countries around the world.

英文譯者簡介

　　戴春馨出生於台灣台北，她在2008年畢業於國立高雄師範大學，並取得英國文學博士學位，現就職於實踐大學高雄校區。主要研究領域為亞裔和非裔文學，現階段正專注於少數族裔作家身份認同方面的研究，主要探討少數族群作家的身份探索。

　　Chuen-shin Tai was born in Taipei, Taiwan. She got her Ph.D. of Arts Degree in English literature from National Kaohsiung Normal University in 2008. She now teaches at Shih Chien University Kaohsiung Campus in Taiwan. Her major field of study is Asian-American and African-American literature. At present, she is working on mapping identities for minority writers.

英文校訂者簡介

　　尼琅菘擁有國立高雄師範大學英語文學博士學位，任職於實踐大學高雄校區，為應用英語學系助理教授。他的研究主要聚焦於詩歌拜倫勳爵和英國浪漫主義。

　　Jon Nichols earned his Ph.D. in English literature from The National Kaoshiung Normal University. He is currently an Assistant Professor within the Department of Applied English at Shih Chien University in Kaohsiung, Taiwan. His research interests center around the poetry Lord Byron and British Romanticism as a whole.

語言文學類　PG2798　台灣詩叢18

金色的曾文溪
The Golden Zengwen River
——方耀乾台漢英三語詩集

作　　者/方耀乾
英語譯者/戴春馨
英語校訂/尼琅菘
叢書策劃/李魁賢（Lee Kuei-shien）
責任編輯/楊岱晴
圖文排版/黃莉珊
封面設計/王嵩賀

發 行 人/宋政坤
法律顧問/毛國樑　律師
出版發行/秀威資訊科技股份有限公司
　　　　　114台北市內湖區瑞光路76巷65號1樓
　　　　　電話：+886-2-2796-3638　傳真：+886-2-2796-1377
　　　　　http://www.showwe.com.tw
劃撥帳號/19563868　戶名：秀威資訊科技股份有限公司
　　　　　讀者服務信箱：service@showwe.com.tw
展售門市/國家書店（松江門市）
　　　　　104台北市中山區松江路209號1樓
　　　　　電話：+886-2-2518-0207　傳真：+886-2-2518-0778
網路訂購/秀威網路書店：https://store.showwe.tw
　　　　　國家網路書店：https://www.govbooks.com.tw

2022年8月　BOD一版
定價：290元
版權所有　翻印必究
本書如有缺頁、破損或裝訂錯誤，請寄回更換

讀者回函卡

國家圖書館出版品預行編目

金色的曾文溪：方耀乾台漢英三語詩集The
Golden Zengwen River / 方耀乾著；戴春馨英
譯. -- 一版. -- 臺北市：秀威資訊科技股份有
限公司, 2022.08
　　面；　公分
BOD版
內容為台語文、中文、英文對照
ISBN 978-626-7088-96-8 (平裝)

863.51　　　　　　　　　　　111010758